Publisher: E. S. E'LAPPELLE'

21st Century Mice: Mazz, Chanders, & Sahara Mouseproud

Mouse illustrations by: Beatriz Bravo Inside cover illustration by: Imogen Lee

Ice cream: copyright Alenakaz, http://www.dreamstime.com/alenakaz_info

Typesetting and editing by: Jennifer Lancaster. www.jenniferlancaster.com.au

Cover Design by: Heather Upchurch, Art & Design Studios

ISBN-13: 978-0-6482637-0-8

A catalogue record for this book is available from the National Library of Australia

Printed in Australia by IngramSpark

21st Century Mice: Mazz, Chanders, & Sahara MouseProud

E. S. E'LAPPELLE'

ABOUT THE AUTHOR

E.S. E'LAPPELLE' has a background in health and enjoys the privilege of being in the medical industry. She lives in the most liveable city in Australia and enjoys stories of humour.

DEDICATION

I dedicate this book to my three nieces and one nephew, who are the inspiration and joy of the stories, and my friends, who support me unconditionally in my creative endeavours: you know who you are and know how much it is appreciated.

In a world full of mischief and adventuring, it's important to realise the enormous potential in everything... especially as mice in the 21st Century.

In everyday Miceness, 21st century mice have an outlook that is somewhat broader, more forward-thinking to 20th century mice. It's edgy, sometimes with clarity as sharp as a knife, sometimes with blurred lines so fuzzy it takes a psychology degree to discover motives.

In a world of pressure that is seen and unseen, with a flurry and lots of scurry, they achieve greatness of character with their own creative style.

Some mice are thinkers, some are doers, some are dreamers, some are all three...

Some love to be in the mix constantly, some value quiet mice time. This is all good, keeping balance when you are this small is important. You don't always have to be the Mouse Boss, sometimes sharing the Miceness around makes things flow very Micely.

The definition of true Miceness is a pure Heart, respect for other mice, older Mice, Ancient Mice, the Micycles we ride and the Mouse havens we live in. This takes great effort and emotional Miceness. But it's worth it.

Occasionally mice may feel Ratty, but remember…Mice are not Rats.

Sometimes we have to be nice to Rats, to help them realise being Mice is nice, but that's where it ends.

A Rat's world is a longwinded set of boroughs, which may never lead anywhere productive.

This can cause Rattiness, angry moods and cranky decisions, therefore creating a big chaotic mess which wears everybody out. Laying the blame on mice so that they achieve less than they would potentially achieve, that's their choice.

Mice know this and are not interested in that way of scurrying. Not Mice at all. When mice know, they just know: that's the truth baby!

Having Mice style is something worthwhile.

The simple adventures in the life of these three extraordinary 21st Century mice will make all of us take notice, take stock, and laugh hard at ourselves. Or at least at myself anyway…

Here are three of the most amazing mice I have met in the vast metropolis of Miceness.

The Sweet Adventures of Mazz, the Lovely

Just a regular day in the fun life of Mazz MouseProud. Grandmouse and Grandpoo were pottering about. Mazz liked to watch her afternoon television. It was her time to catch up on world events, and it was a lovely plan, until one fine day...

"No Grandpoo! Stay away from the television! Olivia is on soon and I don't want to miss it!"

Mazz gained control of the television remote, spreading her arms out, with her crossest expression to ward off the interruption to her afternoon entertainment. Grandpoo would have to wait this time!

Earlier in time, the remote would have been hidden, ever so swiftly, with one quick glance over her little furry shoulder, into her mystery basket where all her treasures lay.

"What is happening with this game; it's not working!?"

After several attempts to master the game of the frog leaping over his lily pad, Mazz showed her cross face. Screwing up her cute little nose, she announced:

"This is Adiculous!"

Singing seemed to be the only thing guaranteed to lift Mazz MouseProud out of a stinky mood: songs from the olden days, songs from the theatre shows, with a lot of jazzy pizazz.

"Aunty, can I sing you a song from the olden days?"

"Sure!"

"Doo doo doo, doo doo dood da lootle doo, the final countdown…doo doo doot dodo… it's the final countdown!...

"Excellent! Do you know any others?", Aunty Clarice asked.

"Sure I do... listen to this one… (her arms began waving in the air).

"I wanna be rich like what's his name, I'll keep the money, you can have the fame! What's yours will soon be mine… I wanna to be kissed from head to toe, by that mouse in the very next row, want a piece of heaven before I die... here comes the 21st century, it's gotta be much better for a mouse like me, I want everything I can, but most of all I want that man! I want that man!"

"Ya ya… you were great, Mazz".

"I know."

"Aunty, can I ask you a question?"

"Sure".

"It's something that's been worrying me, about the olden days, and the day the music died…"

"The day the music died?"

"The mouseicians that passed away, in a plane, leaving that song. Isn't their wives sad?"

"Oh, the song! Of course… Mazz, let me tell you the story and the lesson behind thinking things through properly and assessing all the options… and Mazz, there are always other options…"

Aunty smiled at her sweet-hearted niece.

Driving along in the mousemobile is always an adventure with the MouseProud girls. Mazz watched the scenery go by...

"Stop the Mousemobile!"

"What is going on back there?", Aunt Clarice asked.

"Stop right now. It is a CUBBYHOUSE!"

"We cannot stop for a cubby house Mazz. If you need one, you will have to ask your Papa Mouse -- he needs to buy that".

"mmmmsmmm... please God... cubby house... sandwich... today..."

"What is she doing? Is she praying?", Grandmouse asked incredulously.

"She is bypassing her papa and going straight to the top on this one... obviously".

Visiting Uncle Rad was always a treat. Uncle Rad loves his nieces very much and always has time for surfing adventures.

Uncle Rad had invited the family for a surfing holiday, a fun time for little Mazzi as she loves Uncle Rad and enjoys playing in the water with her snorkel gear.

On arrival to Rad's place, they were greeted by angry snarls from a character foreign to anyone Mazz had met in her life… Quizzing her mother, she looked up and asked, "Is it a cat?"

"No Honey, it's just an angry little dog. We will just leave it alone", Mumma Mouse said. "Meh."

Mazz also spent time with an honorary uncle she called "Macen". Macen is a sporty uncle, with his golf clubs in his pocket and a cheeky wink whenever he saw her.

"Aunty, you are the best! Macen… you are just trouble."

“Huh! There you are Macen, you’re completely sussed out!” Aunty laughed, as it was only too true. Uncle Mace with his cheeky nature, was a troublemouser.

One day, on their way home from the food market, Grandmouse and Mazz were walking along towards the mousehouse when all of a sudden Mazz realised something, something major, something that rarely happened in the mornings at Grandma’s house. This something had stopped Mazz in her little tracks… the green mouse truck was missing?

“I don’t believe it! MACEN WENT TO WORK?” she exclaimed, looking up at her Grandmouse, who was smiling as this was something that rarely happened.

Going with her parents on mousemobile trips to the shopping centre were always fun times. 'Sometimes' foods were Mazzi's favourite. Today she had her mind set on some ice cream!

As she sat in the back, she listened as her mousey parents giggled with each other in conversation. *Righto...* thought Mazz... these two needed a stern warning before moving off.

"Now, you two need to behave or else there will be no ice-cream".

Her chubby little finger was wagging at them, as it does when she needed to make a point.

Walking was something Grandmouse did quite a lot of. She walked everywhere, to save money, to stay healthy, to free up her mind, which was cluttered with all sorts of chores. Mazz loved to dance, sing and skip but walking was just a bit too ordinary for her.

Shopping expeditions were always eventful.

"We are nearly home, just around the corner" smiled Grandmouse.

"Can't we get a taxi?" Mazz protested.

Grandmouse laughed as they walked hand-in-hand towards the Mousehouse.

Collecting things gave Mazz joy. Scrappy bits of this and that found its way into her hands and was stashed away for later use. Fairly soon, the house would be overrun with collections of collectings.

On the way to the big store with Aunty, on a walk (which is her favourite thing to do), Mazz took interest in a long stick. This stick came along for the walk in Mazzi's hands, pointing at things and drawing crosses on the sidewalk every five steps. It became a very long walk.

Once they reached the store, Mazz gave way to tears. What would become of her new-found friend, "stick"? She knew she had to leave it behind to attend the shopping.

"Leave it in this garden and we will collect it on the way out. You must leave the stick outside Lovely", Aunty said.

"OK".

On the way home Grandmouse wondered aloud if Mazz would remember her stick.

"Are you serious? Of course she will remember..."

Aunty knew she would remember her pet stick, and when you know, you know.

"There it is! Hi Stick, Let's go!" Mazz chirped happily, stopping every five steps to draw on the ground with her stick or point at something.

It became an even longer walk than Aunty was expecting. Were they going to get home before dark, she wondered?

“Right, enough with the sticks, we need to get home… and you are going to hurt yourself or someone else with it waving it around like that”.

Mazz kept right along doing what she was previously until it was time to cross traffic. The stick was left to the side as Aunt lead the way.

Mazz turned to Grandmouse, who was trailing behind, to comment:

“I don’t know what it is with Aunt and sticks…but sometimes you need to be nice to sticks…”

Both Grandmouse and Aunt giggled all the way – swiftly – home.

"I am not Cinderella Mouse, or your slave!" Mazz announced to the room.

What had brought this protest on was anyone's guess but Mazz rarely moved from here to there without good reason.

"Sometimes it's good to listen to your mummies and daddies. If your mum asks you to do her job, you can do that job, it is good if you do that job but if daddies ask you to do that job, well... mens can do their jobs theirselves!" Mazzi said philosophically.

Aunty Clarice stood in surprise while Papa mouse smiled and complained that his requests were unjustly overlooked.

Running around the room with a cheeky grin was Mazz, a piece of paper stolen from her Aunty, waving in her hand.

“Do you want this?” she teased Aunt Clarice.

“Give that back Miss, it is for work and I need it!” Aunt chased around Grandmouse’s bed, trying to snatch it back. It was just out of reach as Mazz ran off with it into another room.

“Mazz!! I need it back!”

Mazz stuck her head around the corner waving the paper. “Better find me then...”

Aunt called out, “Oh, you want to play that game? I will play that game but I will win that game”.

With tears streaming down her face from breathless laughing, Aunt rescued her paperwork from a playful niece.

Mazzi sometimes enjoys giving her worldly advice to her elders.

"Aunty Clarice, who looks after you?"

"I do Mazz, why?"

"Where do you live?"

"By myself, near the beach, Mazz"

"You don't live at Grandma's house anymore?"

"No… and when you grow up, you will live somewhere else also, but I imagine not until you are married?"

"Are you marriaged?"

"No, not married".

"Darl, you need to find yourself a nice husband… I already know who I will marry. His name is Joshua; we work togther at kinder..." Mazz says matter of factly.

"If you have a ring, you never let go, no matter what…" she continues, all wise, all knowing, all committed.

"Hee hee. Really? That is lovely Mazz".

It's shower time and the mice need to get soaped up and rinse the dirt of the day down the drain. On go the shower caps and off go the clothes.

"I am naked and in the soaping area!" Mazzi announces.

"The soaping area?", Aunt asked, puzzled.

"Yes, the soaping area, see we soap here, get ready then rinse off… down the drain."

"OK, make sure you wash those pits?"

"Now, we are in the drying area", Mazz announces.

"OK, make sure you dry those pits."

Mazzi's tail was hanging out of the refrigerator while Grandmouse cooked up a storm in the Mouse kitchen.

Aunt was surprised at how far inside the refrigerator Mazz had ventured to find what she had lost. What could be so important to find that all but legs and a tail could be seen?

"Look at this, will you?" Aunty Clarice calls Grandmouse over.

"Mazz, what are you doing?"

"Looking for strawberries!" she replied.

"So Mother, when we were growing up, we had to keep the fridge door closed to keep the cool air in and the food fresh, but Mazz can climb into the fridge in search of strawberries and that is perfectly fine?" Aunty Clarice shook her head. How times change.

Driving along in their mousemobile, Mazzi enjoys her computer game. Papa mouse and Mumma mouse chat away until Papa mouse requires Mazzi's attention.

They are on a scenic drive; she should be seeing how beautiful it is outside, not inside… he wonders.

What are mice coming to today? In love with technology instead of each other?

"Mazz, put that away, in fact, give it to me… I want you to look at the birds out there", he points out.

Mazz took the opportunity to fill the silence with a story, a story that didn't draw a breath for hours. A lovely story involving a doll and her lost shoes, which had everyone entertained until they could no longer handle the enthusiastic, theatrical version given by Mazzi.

Papa mouse then promptly handed the computer back into her little hands and gave up hope that Mazz would become a landscape photographer.

Mazzi has a great time out with her dad, he was as cool as Mouse Fathers go. They did a lot together and fishing was one of those things, except baiting squid with the manky blue, inky gooey stuff that oozed out.

Men can do the squid baiting, Mazzi thought.

Later that night, the Fisher mice came home to tell fishy tales.

"How many fish did you catch Mazz?", Aunty Clarice asked.

"Eleven!" she chirped.

"That is super! How many did father catch?" Aunty inquired.

"Zero". Mazzi said, followed by a prankster giggle.

On School… and Rules

Mazzi MouseProud on her first day back at school, so excited and full of social buzz. Mazz was always happy to learn, but had specific ideas on how this would play out. Her excitement at starting the new school year and experiences was dampened by her parents one morning when they teasingly suggested she would be attending boarding school…

This was not to be the case, just a nasty tease, how could this be? Mazz thought.

Mazzi did not and *would not* be attending boarding school. Who would keep the MouseProud house in order or entertained? Clearly this was not to be.

Could her parents really be so uncaring? Her face was full of woe. This wasn't the end to this conversation, she thought to herself...

"You didn't touch any of your fruit ...that should have been eaten before your biscuits in your school lunch, Mazzi", Grandmouse lectured.

"Grandma, that is your life and this is my life, okay?!"

Mazz looked frustrated, bewildered by the rules put upon her over eating priority choice.

"Grandmouse is crazy..." she said, twirling her finger in a circling motion.

❀❀❀

Sitting in her classroom with all the other little mice, the teacher called the role. "Tilly? Freddy? Max? Bob?"

All replied that they were present and attentive. "Mazz?"

"Bonjour!" was Mazzi's reply. Indeed.

The crowd went wild as the footballers came out to play. The MouseProud family loved their sporting activity and were just as excited to cheer on their teams and favourite players.

"Go Bucks!" cheered Mazzi.

"Go Bodgey!" cheered Mazzi.

"Come on Magpies!" cheered her father.

"Come on Hawks!" cheered her mother.

Grandgrumpy, who was her father's father, was yelling at the football also. Mazzi just loved to stir him up... he despised the Hawks.

Periodically, just to stir up her Grandgrumpy, Mazz would run in and randomly jeer, "Go Bodgey!!"

Mazz didn't really have a favourite player, but to cause a reaction among the mice cheering, why not be contrary?

Mazz was also not one to be told off, regardless of the pecking order.

Mid conversation, it was not unusual for Mazzi Mouse to turn her back on drama and walk calmly into another room, so as not to be affected nor give any notice of the behavioural counsel taking place.

"This is not my drama...", she often said.

Prince Charming...

"Oh Grandmouse, I don't know when I will ever find my Prince?" Mazz sighed. Grandmouse smiled at her little dilemma of the day.

"And how will I ever cope with being a Princess?"

Sitting at the breakfast table Great Grandpoo ate his buttered bread and juice.

"Poppa Freddy! Don't drink that! You will turn into a frog!"

Who took the cheese…?

"Are we stopping for snacks Grandmouse?" Mazz wondered, as she was a tad peckish. *Oh here we are, McCheeseys*. Great!

"I will just have my regular order, thanks Grandmouse?"

The order arrives but it is missing everything but a fluffy white ice cream. Mazz looks in the bag for the mandatory items. No items?

"Here you go Mazzi".

"Umm… where's my cheese?"

"No cheese today honey".

"Cheese swipers…" replied Mazzi.

Carpark church

Driving around in Grandmouse's mousemobile, it was carpark chaos. Rather busy at the shops this morning and there was plenty on their to-do list for the day.

Mazz watched as Grandmouse weaved in and out of the shoppers' car park looking for somewhere to stop. It was hectic all right. Finally, a spot opened up and Grandmouse wasted no time in taking it.

"Oh Thank you God!" Grandmouse said.

"Grandmouse? Did God give you that carpark?"

First Crush

"Aunt, it happened!", Mazz said excitedly.

"What happened, Honey Bunch?", Aunty Clarice asked, smiling away at the cuteness of first crush.

"My first crush on, he has a crush on me. It finally happened, we are crushing on each other".

"Who is this crush on? Bob?"

"No, Milly has a crush on him but he doesn't crush on her. I know this but I don't know if I should tell her. She thinks he does..."

"So who is crushing on you then?"

"Malcom. But what do I do now?"

"I wouldn't say anything at all. If you are all friends, just keep it to yourself and maybe down the road she will crush on someone else. You don't always have to be the one to say something even if you know, you know?"

"Sure!"

On Cooking...

Master Mouse Chef is a stressful occupation and no one takes this more seriously than Mazz and her cousin Chanders MouseProud. The pressure is high, the skill level outstanding, the time limits, ridiculous.

"I don't know how I will cope in that competition?" Mazz is worried.

"Getting these muffins made and cooked to perfection in time just seems impossible!"

"I am sure you would be fine Mazz. Are you going to be a master chef?"

"Yes, so I have to practise my muffins now..."

Rapunzel

Mazzi MouseProud has long, mousey, thick, knotty hair that is rarely brushed by herself... but one day she hopes to have an extraordinarily long braid to swish over her shoulder and out of the palace tower of her imagination...

Eventually the time came for a hair trimming. The negotiation was always going to be intense, Mazz was a tough nut to crack. The brush may even get lost in the mess of hair before cutting anything took place.

Mazz was not about to lose inches; mouse curls would be guarded.

"So, see these bits here, these little bits, just the golden end bits in my fingers?" Mazz instructed her Hair Dresser, Summer.

"Yes..."

"Only the golden bits, thank you".

Mazz watched carefully as the golden tips of the hair endings fell in a feathered pile on the floor.

Miss Fussy-Eater

Dinner time can be challenging for a little mouse household where all mice like different pieces. Grandmouse was fairly adept at variations to keep little mice eating heartily but Mumma mouse was still learning how to negotiate the family menu plan.

It was pasta night, made without Gluten, which can sometimes cause tummy aches for Mice. Sometimes it can be difficult to keep everyone happy. But cheerfully we try.

Mazz was a true food critic, after all she had great plans to be Master Chef Mouse in future. There were clear-cut levels to be achieved.

Handling the pasta between her fingers, wiggling it in the air to show the consistency, "This is the most A'sgusting thing I have ever eaten", Mazz announced to the bench and promptly gave her meal away.

❀ ❀ ❀

Poor Mumma Mouse tries so hard, however there will be times when what one mouse likes another dislikes.

Zucchini is a favourite vegetable for most of us, in moderation, but Mazz was unconvinced.

“Ach! This tastes just like water, I just can’t deal with it”.

“Just two more greens Mazz. Finish your vegetables and consider your day successful”, Grandmouse suggested.

Holiday Fun

Family holidays are fun; especially fishing holidays, or surfing holidays, or motorbike holidays, or island holidays, well just any holidays in the MouseProud clan, as it was adventure time!

On an Island holiday, mouse carts were the only transport available… steep hills, palm trees, beaches and canoes. So much fun to be had by all.

Mazz loved this holiday as everyone was travelling together. She was the first to hop into one of the carts.

"All aboard!" she announced.

"Quick GrandPoo, we need to get past them, faster!" Glee filling her eyes, GrandPoo overtook the other family carts on the hill, while Papa was still way behind.

"See you later!" said Mazzi cheekily.

Papamouse overtook the following carts on the next hill.

"See you later!" he voiced cheekily.

❁ ❁ ❁

On a smaller, family weekend, the MouseProuds followed the coastline to Cheeseland, a famous cheese town full of factories that made all sorts of cheeses.

Mazzi had been dreaming beautiful dreams of candy cane cheese pops, cheesy vegemite sticks, strawberry cheese cakes, chocolate cheese donuts, cheese sauces to suit everyone… for the cheesy pizza scrolls calling her name.

“We are starving Honey, the little mice need feeding or they will be wailing for hours and no one wants that to happen”, Mumma said.

“Hmmm well then, let’s see where we can stop along the way. I am sure there will be something to suit everyone?”

Poppa stopped to have a look around. That restaurant looked pleasant, he thought to himself. He walked in and booked a dining table for the family as his little girls needed to eat or pandemonium would break out.

“We have a table Mumma, let us eat”.

On entry to the restaurant, Mumma noticed they may have been underdressed. Holiday clothes were not suitable for this lovely establishment; not something obvious to Poppa.

But they were hungry and her little misses were very polite and well-behaved as they had always eaten in different places, trying new dishes at each stop.

Mazz, accustomed to ordering her favourite dishes, spoke to the manager.

"Just a Queen of Hearts and a mini Cappucino thanks?"

Normally her favourite outing involved pancakes and coffee at the local Pancake Palace. (Oh what a treat, out with Grandmouse).

That was the usual treat on a ladies' day out, but this was holidays and a luncheon. The manager was happy to take her order and bring her favourite milky chino on the table.

All were pleased with their meals and although Mumma Mouse was wishing they had dressed more for the occasion, it was good to have a full belly of nutritious food.

The manager was keen to see his diners were happy with the service and food. "How is everything here? Are the meals satisfactory?", he asked with a smile.

"Lovely, thank you". Poppa Mouse thanked the manager for such attentive customer service.

"That was the best cheese I have ever eaten!" Mazz praised.

"I am glad you liked it". The Manager smiled at this audacious little mouse, as she had made his day!

All MouseProuds jumped into their mousemobile and headed out to the next stop in their adventure. This would involve soft pillows and comfy beds.

What a full weekend!

Little Sisters...

Little sisters can be hard work. They have to have everything you have and then they sometimes hand it back in less than perfect condition. The really good little sisters take over your socks and underwear drawer, claiming those items are theirs when clearly they are not.

"You are too small!" Mazzi told Sahara. "You cannot play with that as you are too small! That is only for grown up girls, not babies".

Sahara was not fussed; there were plenty of her sister's things to explore, so she crawled swiftly onto the next. To which she was promptly told that she was also too small to play with that item.

It was a bonnet for the parade that became the casualty of the week. The drama to unfold would forever draw a line in the sister sand.

Giggles and mischief pulled at all the bonnet ornaments, the feathers and ribbons pulled apart, the glitter decorating the floor. Mazzi's bedroom, a crime scene...

"NOOOOOO!!! Mumm!!!!! Get them out of my room!!" Mazz cried out.

Mumma mouse heard this alarming scream and made her way to the bedroom.

What she found were two cheeky little mice inside a pile of colourful mess and a distraught Mazzi crying as loud as she could. Nothing could appease this girl from the betrayal before her. Her Bonnet, beautifully put together with love, from her craft afternoon with Papamouse… all gone.

"Look what they did!!"

"Honey they are only toddlers; they don't know what they are doing." Mumma MouseProud defended.

"They are NOT toddlers! They know what they are doing. This is OUTRAGEOUS! Get out of my room!" Mazz was inconsolable.

She stayed in her room collecting the remnants of her bonnet, mad as fury. Later her conversation was calmer but just as definite in intention.

"I think from now on there should be no more yelling in the house, no more corner time or no counting, except for Sahara because she may need it." Mazz addressed the room with certainty.

"And just as a new General Rule, I think I should be the child boss", she added.

"Really now?"

"Yes, really."

"Well how about we stick to the first general rule, where you mice behave, therefore I won't have to count or raise my voice or send you to the corner to think. And no, you cannot act as the child boss." Mumma was unphased by the new policy on behaviour suggested.

"OH COME ON?!"

Helping Out

"Mazzi, come inside now, it is your nap time."

"Can't come in now, we are working here."

Mazz followed Papa Mouse around the mousemobile, vigilantly helping him wash the tyres.

She was a busy little mouse and liked to help out where possible, including washing her Aunty Clarice's mouse truck. Using a toilet brush was not what Aunt had in mind… as she cared to keep the paint *on* the vehicle… but Mazz assured her, Mumma would replace it, not to worry, everything was fixable.

Fixing things was a great pastime in the MouseProud House, or 'bixing things' as Mazz was prone to say.

"Papa is a bixer (fixer), that's what he does, who he is, how it is. We are bixing things here… he has been down the hardware store for hours buying up tools and supplies. Why you ask? That is because he is a bixer (fixer)."

No job was too hard for Mazz, except if stairs were involved and then second thoughts as to whether that one more thing was worth the drop of sweat off her freckled face.

A special request...

"Can I tell you something?"

"Sure Mazz, what do you want to tell me?"

"My back is sore; can you massage it Aunty? Just the soft way, not the flicks…" Mazz motioned with her hands.

"OK, not the flicks, just a relaxing one, for how long?"

"A few minutes."

"The left leg." "And the other left leg…"

"And some more minutes…"

"Ok, has that helped free things up?"

"Hmmm… yes…very good".

Swimming practice lessons are a fantastic activity for little mice to take up. The MouseProuds are avid swimmers, attending swimming school twice a week. Mazz seemed to go up a level quite regularly. She was particular on her favourite instructors also.

Mazzi's miceness was always popular; she just enjoyed life to the full and got the most out of whatever activity she was into doing.

Time had come for a level change. As always, Mazz was nervous on her performance yet always exceeded her expectations. The instructor gave her commendations and let her gently know that a new instructor would be needed. Mazz was sure she did not want the male instructor assigned to the next level so she began negotiating, as is her way most of the time.

"Mazz, what if I check out the list of instructors and if I think they will be good for you, I will put you in that class with him?" her current instructor reasoned.

"Um… I would prefer not" was Mazzi's reply. Definite in her preference for the instructor she was happy with.

In the end, she was assigned to a female instructor of her choice.

All day long, the 'wanna be child boss' nagged her father, ignored his requests, argued the point, procrastinated on any subject that involved tidying, cleaning, or sorting her own areas. It was a tired father MouseProud standing before his eldest mouse when he sternly stood his ground.

"Are you serious? You are going to spend some time cleaning up that toy room and your bedroom. How many times have I asked you to get it out of the way?"

Quick as a flash, she answered him with yet another excuse as to why this request of his could not take place.

"Do not speak to me in that tone, thank you Miss", Father spoke strongly.

"Well!... rahha rahhh", Mazz replied.

"Mazz, there is no need for you to get upset, just do what you have been asked please?" Aunty Clarice had seen and heard enough agro for the day.

"Oh I am not upset... HE IS JUST CRACKING IT." (She says over her shoulder, walking towards her overflowing toy kingdom).

"How do you answer that?", her father asked.

"I wish I knew?" Aunty answered.

Doctors always had Mazzi's attention; they had all the answers and gave much appreciated attention to a little mouse with a lot of allergies.

Mazz is quite popular at the local Doctors, often seen running around the clinic, into areas marked 'staff only', chatting to everyone, smiling, charming with her enthusiasm. No one would suspect there was anything needing medical attention on this mouse as she skipped and chirped merrily.

It was her turn to be called in. Grandmouse carried her little grandmouse in to see Dr. Cheesey.

"Hello Doctor!" Mazz was happy to see Doctor Cheesey as regularly as she did.

"What seems to be the problem Mazz?"

"She has a sore leg Doctor, a bit of a breathing issue and a cough that keeps hanging around. Not eating much at the moment. We are not sure what to do?" Grandmouse said.

"Ok then, let us listen to this chest then and see what's going on."

"Thank you Doctor!"

Mazz was a very cooperative patient, breathing in and out when asked, sticking her tounge out, letting the little light in her ears, as this was all Doctor procedure. She knew because she had a doctor's set at home. The next step was to check her temperature... if he forgot that, she would remind him.

Satisfied that her check-up was fully carried out by her favourite Doctor, they set off home until the next time – which would be sooner rather than later – took place.

❀ ❀ ❀

The next favourite place for Mazz to visit was the 'Mouse Hosteo' as she called it. Hosteo is translated as 'Hospital' for regular mice.

With all the possible allergies that could affect the lovely little mouse, there were several visits to the hospital and a worried set of parents wondering how bad this allergy could be. Was it something in the house? Is it more than an allergy to cats? What could it be?

Mazz lay in the huge hospital bed, wrapped up like a cocoon, waiting for the Doctor to attend.

A perfect patient lays there serenely, allowing the nurses to fluff her pillows for comfort, change her drinking water and check her temperature as that is procedure according to her Doctors set… and then let the Doctor decide on the pink medicine she must take.

The Doctor was finally here, with other doctors by her side. Surrounded by doctors, Mazzi knew it was all good. This is what it should always be: one thousand percent medical attention. Dr Cheesey knew what he was doing.

"Hello Doctor!" Mazz greeted happily, all signs of weakness disappeared.

Her parents often wondered if the medical staff thought they had white clouds for brains. Was this mouse seriously ill? Did she look ill at that point? No, clearly. Hours before was another story.

Another favourite pastime was to hide the television remote from Grandpoo. He always loved that...

Many an argument took place when items of practical use were hidden in such special hiding places, that only a little mouse could recall. Emptied tissue boxes of all tissues and placed each tissue on all her dolls in the lounge; tea towels from Grandmouse's kitchen drawers, for various tasks, mainly because her plastic babies were sleeping in-between tea parties.

A peachey-colored blur ran past a doorway into another room.

"What was that?", Aunty Clarice asked.

"I suspect an underwear thief?" Uncle James supposed.

Grandpoo and Mazz quite often had a difference of opinion where possessions were concerned.

Just as he believed everything under his roof – whether he purchased it or not – was his, so did she. This caused great contention where daily television programs were concerned, or her grandmother: her time, her attention.

It was morning time and Grandmouse's routine was standard: breakfast, clean up, play time.

Mazz had enjoyed her breakfast of bread and cheese, but had taken to helping Grandmouse wash up afterwards. If Grandmouse was not present, Mazzi would clear cups herself. Although she could not reach the sink, if she balanced the cups on the top of the bench, on tippy toes, pushed the cups over the side, they were in, ready to be cleaned or thrown out into the bin after becoming chipped from the fall.

It was during one of these cleaning up routines that Grandpoo questioned the goings-on in the kitchen.

"What are you doing in there?", he asked.

With eyes barely seeing over the benchtop and with a wave of a little stick finger came the reply. "Just eat your breakfast".

Mazz was on a mission to clean, with no interruptions from Grandpoo.

❁ ❁ ❁

Another day, all of Grandpoo's socks, singlets, handkerchiefs and undershorts lay on the floor outside of the cabinet they once rested in; once folded, once ready for the next day of wearing.

How happy Grandpoo will be when he comes home to find it all thrown over the shoulder of his Grandmices or worn as head pieces around the house!

Hair-raising...

"Can we brush your hair Aunty?", Mazz asked.

"Sure."

All three mice, Mazz, Chanders and Sahara, found hair brushes and started to brush. At times they strained the friendship with their heavy-handed hair-dressing styling.

"Gentle Sahara, please, that is hurting my scalp", Aunty said.

"Aunty, I just need to get a tie for the back. We will style it for you, just lovely". Mazzi was happy… she found it relaxing when Aunt brushed her long hair so she enjoyed returning the favour and creating something wild that would suit her favourite Aunty.

After more brushing, teasing, plaiting, and scalp scratching, Mazzi tried to change direction and release one of the plaits. The hair seemed to be knotted. How with all that brushing it could knot was anyone's guess but soon Mazz would fix the dilemma.

"I will be back in a minute Aunty. Just wait here", she said.

Not a minute later, Mazz was back in hair styling mode and ready to take on this knotted hair clump.

'Snip, snip, snip'

Aunty heard the scissors cutting through the back of her hair… Mazz was quick to remedy the situation. Coming around to face her shocked Aunt with a clump of hair wrapped around a hair tie in one hand and blue scissors in the other, she calmly explained:

"There was no other way…"

Aunty let out a small shriek at the sight of her hair and the vision of what the back of her head could look like…

"Mum!!!", Aunty Clarice called.

"Am I in trouble?", Mazz asked worriedly.

"Hee hee, it's all right, no trouble, don't you stress... MUM!!?

In the end, the hair would grow back.

Mazz needed to vent, this was getting "ADICULOUS!"

"No one in my house appreciates my work! My mother doesn't care about my work or even look at it, she just says to pin it up on my door or she throws it out in the bin!"

Mazzi's statement was full of artistic rejection. Creating all of these bits of paper were sacred and individual, couldn't she see that? Was there no vision? Artistic suffering would have to be endured until she was old enough for a studio.

Clean-up time

"Mum always gives me two dollars to clean my room", Mazzi replied to Aunt Clarice on a requested clean-up on an overflowing toy kingdom.

"It is your room and your things, money doesn't need to be paid for you to look after your own things and keep them tidy" said Aunty Clarice.

"That is Mumma's Rules!" Mazzi cried.

"I am not your Mumma, Aunt's rules are very different and I am saying I will not be paying you. It is up to you to look after your things"...

After mumblings and ramblings from a disgruntled niece sitting on the floor in amongst her toys, there was a look of annoyance on Mazzi MouseProud's face. One more argument may win this debate.

"How about we pack it all up and send it to mice that have nothing and would be only too happy to keep things in order? Then you won't have to worry about cleaning up or your two dollars." Aunt was unimpressed and not about to lose the argument.

"Hmmmm..." Mazz mumbled and proceeded slowly around the room, adjusting small things.

At Grandmouse's house all was quiet, too quiet. Mazz wondered where her much, much older Great GrandPoo was?

Where was he today on such a beautiful sunny day? The question just had to be asked.

"Grandmouse, where is old Great GrandPoo?"

"He did wake up early this morning, came out to the kitchen to make a cup of hot cheese and then announced he would be going back to his mouse hole to sleep…"

"Bad decision…" Mazz MouseProud decreed.

There were two little mice chatting in a corner playfully, discussing life and books of interest with the greatest of enthusiasm when along came Dummell, a ratty little mouse having an unhappy moment at Mouse School.

"SHOOSH UP! YOU ARE WAY TOO LOUD!" he pinioned at the lovely mice in the corner enjoying their chat.

"Excuse me? We are discussing these books here", Mazzi MouseProud answered, unsure as to why one couldn't express these thoughts particularly as they were sitting in the book corner; where else?

"You need to be quiet." Dummell was getting bossier by the minute.

"We do not need to shoosh, so you should just calm it" was Mazzi's short reply.

The two mice carried on in the book corner, discussing books with enthusiasm – as that is clearly the place for it.

The Swift Adventures of Chanders the Great

Chanders MouseProud: "What a beautiful day!" Chanders looked around, gazing lovingly at her surroundings.

Chanders MouseProud always noticed the little things, the things that most people overlooked. Specific and detailed in her mannerisms, beautiful as she was smart – which was limitless if you asked her Aunt Clarice.

In the everyday, young Chanders is a flurry of energy, talking faster than a rabbit munches lettuce.

Out shopping with Grandmouse, the toy section became a hive of activity, pulling things off the shelves: she just had to have them, it was life imperative!

"I just need this!", she said as it went in the trolley. Grandmouse was unconvinced.

"Oh Grandmouse, I just have to have it!"

"Really?"

"Oh Pulleeeaasssee Grandmouse! I must have it!"

Chanders, a sporty kind of mouse, was happy to try her hand at whatever sporty activity her parents were into or suggested.

Golf was a pastime of her PappyMouse. They would practise their swing in the yard, ever so professional.

"Are you sure you know how to play golf, Papa?"

"Sure I do, like this.."

"Mmm… let me show you how to hit the ball, just like this!"

Ever the expert, a natural sports mouse, happy to instruct in her chirpy way.

"Are you sure you know what you are doing?"

"Are you sure you know where we are going?"

"Are you sure you know how to dance? (Grandmouse does a jig). "Oh No! That is NOT DANCING… Grandmouse just STOP! Let me show you how to dance".

"Are you sure you know how to do that?"

This line of questioning would be a challenge to the everyday person but not to Chanders. She may end up on an interrogation team working the perps till they crack… "Are you sure you only boosted two MouseMobiles…?"

Chanders loved to join in on games, but today her Papee was doing his exercise training.

'Mouseups' were a fully immersing exercise but Chanders couldn't keep her feet on the ground. Quick-thinking Chanders pondered for seconds before shouting:

"Quick Papa, hold my legs!"

This was no easy feat as Chanders was a tiny little mouse with tiny, tiny ankles. Away she went, perfecting her 'Mouseups' to build huge, mini-abdominals.

"Are my cousins here? I want to play with them".

"Sure Honey, they will be here soon, how was your day?", Grandmouse asked.

"Mmm it was good".

"What did you do today?"

"Well I had lunch and watched television".

"What did you watch?"

"My Crobrams…"

"Your Crobrams?" Grandmouse was suspect.

"Yes, my television crobrams (programs)".

❀ ❀ ❀

Chanders sat in front of her television crobrams (programs), flicking through the channels… looking puzzled and annoyed at the same time.

Days earlier, she had been discussing television world with her Papa. They often chat about the olden days as her cousin Mazzi liked to reminisce. They conversed about a hero of her papa's… his name was "Danger Mouse", hero to the people.

Chanders was quite impressed with the heroics of "Danger Mouse" and it must have stayed on her mind for a few days.

"Come on!!!!"

"Is everything allright Honey?", Papa asked.

"I cant find it…"

"What can't you find?"

"The Crobram (program) … Emergency Mouse (AKA Danger Mouse)".

Chanders is a thinker, always pondering, questioning specifics… yet when questioned by her parents it was not her practice to reply with a "yes" to requests.

"Is 'NO' the only answer you can say?", Her father asked.

"No..." she answered.

Chanders loved roadtrips and her parents obliged as they often enjoyed the same. Let's go here and there, see this and that, buy this or those, as long as it's quality.

All dressed in pink and fluffy, Chanders buckled in for a long family trip to the country to meet some country mice and their big pet chickens.

"Can we feed the chicken?", she asked excitedly.

"If Uncle says so, sure".

Hours went by in the mousemobile, the land was green and full on large mountains, boy there was so many mountains. Trees, mountains, giant birds, everything looks massive in a little mice world.

"Are we nearly at the chickens, as this is Boring!?" chirped a little mouse from the back seat of the mousemobile.

Aunty Clarice giggled; not enough stimulus in the world for this one.

Aunty Clarice worked a lot, but while she worked she thought about her audacious nieces, often smiling to herself and telling stories of their adventures to her mouse friends and mouse workers.

One day in particular, Aunty thought she should telemouse Grandmouse to see how all was going…

“Hello there, how are things?”, she asked.

“Good!” was the reply.

“Do you have Chandeliers with you today?”

“Yes, it’s lots of fun…”

(Grandmouse, turning to someone else in the room) “Please get down off the bed Honey!”

In the background, Aunt could hear some little comments.

“Can you please stop jumping on that?!”

“Tee hee hee hee...” came the reply.

“She is swinging from the lamp shades, isn't she?” Aunt was smiling.

“Ahhhh not quite…” Grandmouse was somewhat preoccupied.

“I am Jumping on the bed!!” Chanders announced.

This could possibly be one of her favourite things to do, exuding joy and happiness and jumping on the bed.

Chanders skipped, jumped, exaggerated her stride, bounced, but rarely stood still.

Many things on the go and in her hands, she raced into the room, missed the table with her utensils, and hit her head on the corner – followed by a large cry. Chanders only knew one way to cry, really loudly.

"What happened in here?" Grandmouse came rushing in at the sound of cries.

"She was trying to do too much at once, lost concentration trying to climb the chair with her hands full, and hurt herself", Aunt explained.

"I hurt myself… boo hoo hoo".

"Okay Honey, we need to slow right down, doing one thing at a time".

"Pardon?"

"Running in the kitchen with your hands full, causes trouble. Then you tried to jump on the chair before putting anything down. So next time, you walk into the kitchen, put what is in your hands on the table and then climb up on the chair to the table... yes?"

"Yes".

Later that night while all changing into mousewear for bed, two little mice were on Grandma's bed chatting away when Chanders came in, emptying her hands by throwing it all on top of the bed and then launching herself from the ground onto the bed. That is how you do it.

"Progress", Aunt thought.

A loud cry came from the kitchen again. Grandmouse ran in to investigate. "What happened?"

Great GrandPoo watched on and then relayed the events to GrandMouse. "She ran straight into the table and knocked her head".

"I hit maaaaa heeaaadd… boo hooo hoo hoo". Chanders held her eye.

"Right, what have I said? No running in the kitchen, Mazzi. What did Grandmouse say?"

"No running in the kichen.."

"Good, Chanders? What did Grandmouse say?"

"Noooo Ruuuunnnniiing in the Kiittccchhheeen..."

"Good, Sahara? What did Grandmouse say?"

"Ummm, I don't know?" was Sahara's reply. All laughed at Sahara missing the cue.

"What did Grandmouse say about running in the kitchen?"

"Ummm... Nothing!" Sahara replied.

Always hands on, Chanders liked to get what she needed done, quickly. Let's not muck around, time is money so they say. Feeling a bit under the weather, she searched for her vaporiser.

Puff, Puff, Puff and it's all better. Breathing easier, she put the lid back on and tried to place it all back in its box.

"Please put the medicine away Chanders, we have things to do."

"I am trying… it's just impossible!!!"

As always, Chanders is questioning rules and regulations, looking for a loophole or a clarification.

"How am I supposed to talk when I have to be quiet?"

This is a conundrum.

It was not unusual for Chanders to be independent in her thinking and activities. One of her favourite statements to Aunty when she tried to help her put her coat on was to say:

"I can do it by my own!"

Aunty was happy to oblige and impressed at Chanders' willingness to learn and challenge herself to achieve what needed doing. She was not a helpless little mouse that was lazy in shoelace tie-ups, that was for sure.

"Sure Honey Bunch, good job", Aunty replied.

The playhouse kitchen ran like a well-oiled machine, there were pots and pans and cups 'o' tea for all when the three kind mice were busy.

Dressed in her pink apron and Chef's hat, Chanders was in her element, industriously bossing her cousins around and catering to the imaginary customers in her sweet little café.

"What is happening here?", Aunt asked.

"Look Aunt, I am a Microwave" was the answer.

Aunt wondered if she should be a little worried about her niece turning into a microwave? Interesting concept.

Aunty liked to purchase little gifts for her nieces that could be fun all-year-round and at any time, so she bought all three nieces a tin tea set with its own little spotty case. Tea parties were on trend; everyone wanted a tea party and the MouseProuds were no exception.

"Thank you sooo much for my tea set Aunty!"

Chanders was sweet, as always. "Of course darling, I am happy to do that for you. Have a lovely time OK?"

"OK then, thank you".

Then it was back to making as much noise as possible, with Sahara in the background instructing her Grandmouse to "Shoosh!"

"Don't you Shoosh me!" Grandmouse giggled at the feisty mice.

Out in the backyard Chanders and Aunty kicked the ball to each other across the green grass.

Back and forth it went, till fatigue set in and a few kicks weren't exactly precise. This of course would be noticed and corrected by sporty Chanders.

"Like this Aunty… see?!" Chanders gave the ball an almighty kick across the yard straight to her favourite Aunt.

Aunt kicked the ball back best she could.

"Are you sure you know how to play this game?", Chanders asked seriously.

"Huh?"

"Don't HUH me!" was Chanders reply.

Grandmouse's house is a mousey paradise full of treats and adventures. On a trip to the store, the conversation was about Chanders' Papee.

"So, your Papa will be coming later to pick you up after he is finished playing Golf today. So we will bring this shopping home and finish all the chores for the day." Grandmouse chatted lightly to her little ballerina mouse.

"Grandmouse, Papa is not playing golf… he is having a Golf Lesson!" Chanders was specific about the playing and learning aspect of it all.

"…on the golf course, with a qualified instructor, with personalised clubs made to suit all standard course requirements according to world golf policies, etc etc."

It was best to always have the categories straight before conversing with Miss Chanders.

Nighttime Dramas

Bedtime… something necessary for all little mice to do so that more fun can be had the next day when all are rested.

Chanders took her time settling into bedtime. It wasn't something a hyperactive little mouse really wanted to do, with so many things to see and do, soo sooo much fun to have, sooo many treats to eat… but Papa mouse tucked his little daughter into her pink bed and wished her a good night's sleep. Just as he would close the door behind him, he would hear a little voice call out.

"My hair tie has fallen out of my hair and onto the floor! I need it" came the cry.

So around her Papee turned to find the hair bobble so all would be well again.

"I need a drink of water… I am very thirsty" came another request from Chanders MouseProud. So around her Papee turned, to bring her a glass of water.

"How was your doctor's appointment today?"

"It went well today. Honey, is there anything else?"

"Umm…what is Mumma doing?"

"She is cleaning the clothes right now and then we are all going to bed, as we need to rest. Tomorrow is a big day, so good night, sweet dreams".

"Okay. I love you, dad".

"I love you too".

☾ ☾ ☾

"Dad! Dad! Dad?" Chanders called out in the night to her father.

Her father woke to her calling and looked at the mouse clock. In mouse time it was three o'clock in the early hours of the morning. What is the matter with Chanders, he wondered? Did she need water? Having a nightmare? Cold? It had been a cold winter…

"What is it Honey? Are you thirsty?", he inquired.

"I need a foot massage".

"A foot massage hey?" he smiled at her tenacious nature. "My hands are sore already, how about a tummy massage?"

"OK then".

She was happy and content to drift off to sleep and dream of strawberry cupcakes once again.

A New Little Brother

Chanders MouseProud skipped merrily about. She skipped everywhere with a little bounce in her piggy tails. Very pleased with herself, her Princess Mouse room in her Mouse Castle, and a fresh little friend in the form of a new brother to annoy, I mean adore, all day long.

Up in her baby brother's cheeky face, she cooed and sang while he laughed happily at her attention. He thought she was amazing as did everyone else.

"I am your big sister! Do you love your big sister? I will sing you a song", she chirped right up in his face.

Previously, the wait for her new little friend had been tedious. 'How long must we wait?' she asked regularly.

"Mumma Mouse proud always sleeps! She sleeps in the morning, she sleeps in the afternoon, she sleeps at night… she is always asleep!" She voiced her frustrations to her father, who listened with earnest as always.

"Yes Mumma is tired because she is carrying the baby mouse and when he is born she may well be even more tired, which means we will have to help her with him."

"…OH, I am going to be sooo exhausted…" replied Chanders MouseProud.

The cold and flu season was here and it was a doozey! Not in many years had mice suffered so with the coughs and aches of the dreaded rat flu virus. It sent many mice to bed unwell and their families to look after them for at least a few weeks at a time.

During this time, Chanders rested, often having her temperature tested and continuous fluids. When sick, well that is what the body does, it rests, and boy did Chanders sleep! So much so that she went to bed early one of those days, very unwell and when she woke up, she looked out the window, expecting to see a lovely sunlit day but instead she noticed it was not...

"When did it get dark?", she asked her parents.

"Oh Honey, you slept all day and the sun has gone to sleep now as well".

Chanders and father were the best of friends, she liked it when he picked her up from places such as day care, kinder, Nannies house. SHE was usually incredibly tired by this time and was quietly thinking mouse thoughts.

Driving along in the car with her father, he tried to chat with her about her day; he loved to hear what adventures she got up to.

"So, how was your day, what did you do?", he asked cheerfully. Chanders' dad was almost always in a cheerful mood as he was a good-humoured Mouse Father, not a grumpy grouch like some dads.

"Dad, I am sucking my tum (thumb), I am very tired, and can't you see I am resting?" "Well, OK then, you rest up".

Later on, on another pick-up, her father sensed she was very quiet, unusual for Chanders, who chatted away about many subjects she has noticed throughout the week.

In the back of the Mousemobile, Chanders plotted her next activity. So much to do, so little time.

"How was your day, Honey?"

“Good”.

“What did you do today?”

“Just keep your eyes forward and watch the road” was her answer to her puzzled father.

“What are you doing back there?”

“Don’t look, just drive with your eyes on the road…” Chanders was clearly in no mood to chat. Maybe this was the exhaustion she often complained about.

Craft was big with all the MouseProud mice but especially Mazzi and Chanders. They loved cutting things with huge scissors, pasting, painting, colouring, kneading, squashing and Chanders just loved gluing. Boy, did she enjoy gluing things together or onto other things. This could go on for hours or until there was no glue left to glue anything with.

For hours, with craft bits and pieces all over her Papa Mouse's lounge room, her activity looked hectic.

"I need you to put the glue down and tidy all this up Chanders" Mumma said.

Chanders continued on doing what she was doing as if not hearing the suggestion as valid at this time.

Once again, her mother requested the activity to cease. Once again she was rebuffed, making a request for more glue, and it continued back and forth until her Mouse Dad pointed out that there was too much glue applied to things and it was becoming almost ridiculous. The coffee table was starting to suffer.

Aunty Sam tried to settle Chanders' affinity with glue down but still Chanders insisted there were still more things to cut up and glue if she could only have more glue to work with.

Aunty MouseProud chuckled at her feisty niece and her persistence but worried there may be a trip to the Mousepital Emergency Room if this kept going. So she said:

"Any more glue and it is possible that you may accidently stick that to your head and you know what, I am not going to be taking you to hospital. So it will just have to stay stuck to your head until you are old enough to drive yourself there, OK miss?"

Chanders looked at her Aunt in wonder, her little mind visualised this picture and she laughed, shaking her head.

"Stuck to my head… heheheheehe" she chuckled. The craft soon was tidied and the subject of glue (till next time) was quietened.

At Grandmouse's house, all the grand mice enjoyed working on projects in the kitchen. This could be cooking, colouring, reading aloud or play-dough rolling and kneading. Play-dough was great; mixing all the colours into the colour of poo was one of Sahara MouseProud's favourite things to do. Smashing it together, rolling it and flattening it into a stack, like pancakes.

"Hilarious..." Sahara said, admiring her work.

When Grandpoo is away the mice will play. Noise can be made, havoc can be wreaked and Grandmouse has little volume control.

"It's all right Sahara, Pop is away... we can make as much noise as we like. Yay!" enthused her sister.

"Hahahahahaha yay!!", shrieked Sahara.

"Quick, the monsters are coming...run!!!"

"AHHHHH the monsters..."

“There are no monsters in Grandmouse’s house, settle the voices thank you”, Grandmouse said, raising her eyebrows at her cheeky grand mice.

Back at the kitchen table was play-dough time and the contrasting creations were evident.

Chanders made pretty blue, pink and green creations, which ultimately became a bright dough casserole.

She proudly announced her casserole to Aunty.

“Look Aunty, my casserole!” Chanders said, looking happy and proud

“That’s awesome, the best casserole I have ever seen!”

“It’s Play-dough…”

Chanders had to specifically describe it, just in case Aunty thought it was the edible kind. You just never could tell as Aunty got very enthusiastic about creative things she made.

Papa was calling out to little Chanders who was bobbing around the place as she did. FINALLY Papa caught up with her and mouse to mouse asked the important question...

“Did you hear what I just asked you? Are your ears turned on?”, Papa Mouse inquired.

“One of them is turned on and the other one is turned off” was Chanders witty reply.

“So is the one that is turned on listening to me?”, Papa mouse asked.

“I told you, it’s turned off...”

The Sassy Adventures of Sahara the Feisty

Sahara MouseProud was funny. She was also beautiful, creative, discerning and atrociously behaved, all in the same minute…

That is how it seemed to her favourite Aunty Clarice anyhow. Her nieces could make her laugh till her belly ached and the tears from her laughter could fill a bucket!

How special it was to be in the little MouseProud's presence and what was life before them? Fairly dull, she had to concede and yet their life had never, ever been boring.

Sahara's four-year-old mouse self flounced around, giggling, burping, bossing, popping off, all the while generally making blunt and sometimes totally random statements. She issued comments and funny sayings that made the MouseProud family laugh till they cried and proud to the heart.

Sahara was her own mouse, beat to her own drum and kept a sensible nature most of the time, but there was one vice. To her life is a big game… a fun game. You never quite knew what the cheeky little mouse might say or do next… she was a true mystery mouse.

Her mother would quite often say it was just as well she was cute or she would be going to an orphanage.

No way! The Orphanage would have too much fun, Aunty Clarice thought quietly.

"Can I help you hang out the clothes Aunty?"

"Sure! Come on", Aunty said to her beautiful little Lovely.

"I will have hold the pegs… it's a peg shop". Sahara was playing the shopping game.

"Great! I will need four pegs, thank you" Aunty said, trying to get her clothes hung out quickly.

Sahara handed her Aunt four pegs, then another four pegs, yet another four pegs, then four more pegs.

"May I please have another four pegs?", Aunty asked.

"No, as the peg shop is closed!" Sahara announced while running away with the very large peg bucket.

After a lot of negotiation, Sahara agreed to handing out pegs one at a time only as needed, with instruction on how to hang certain items on Grandmouse's clothes line.

"Finally! It is done, let us go back inside to Grandmouse…"

"Yes", Sahara agreed and then proceeded to come up with another game.

The ice cream shop was clearly Sahara's favourite shop-keeping role.

Unfortunately for Aunty, this ice cream business was quite limited in flavours and stock. In Sahara MouseProud's ice cream stall, you could only buy vanilla, pronounced manilla, mint, chocolate and strawberry, and only one ice cream per customer. So if you dropped it, 'too bad, too sad' as Sahara would often say.

"Do you want to buy an ice cream?"

"Why yes, may I have a caramel scoop with a chocolate scoop?"

"We don't sell caramel here, sorry!"

"Well, can I have a mint scoop then?"

"Sorry, no, we just ran out..."

"How about strawberry then?"

"Sorry, no, we just ran out..."

"What kind of shop is this? Do you have any ice cream at all?" Aunty was at a loss as to what kind of shop wouldn't have all the flavours of the rainbow?

"What do you have in flavours then?"

"Manilla. And you can only have one per customer, so if you drop it, well too bad, too sad".

"Really now… Well, three scoops in one cone, thank you miss mousey".

"No problem, here you go. That will be one sugar cube?"

"One sugar cube just for you and by the way, how is your imaginary friend Lupin?"

"Oh yes, well he is good. His business is over the way, but I just do not think I can run this shop and have a partner at the same time, I am just so so busy" Sahara said.

Aunty laughed at her audacious niece. Even an imaginary friend was taking up unnecessary energy in her play life.

It was never easy to keep the tiny mouse's toy room clean, overflowing with everything that was the colour pink and purple.

Dolls, paper scraps, books, costumes, pencils that glowed in the dark, tiny figurines that Aunty likes to suck up in the vacuum cleaner… but that is another story.

Grandmouse's house was a lot like this toy room, the land of the free where biscuits and cheese reigned supreme. But even Grandmouse was having to put in effort to keep some order in the house.

"Sahara! Go clean the toys in the lounge area please Darling, before you go home", she called out. A little voice from somewhere under the dolls answered:

"No, I can't Grandmouse".

"Sahara, you go put the toys away or you are not playing with them next week when you come back to Grandmouse's House!"

"I cannot hear what you are saying Grandmouse…"

“Cheeky corner time then?” Sahara’s father called out. He was not pleased when Grandmouse’s requests were not obeyed and was very quick to let his tiny mice babies know when a line had been crossed.

“I cannot hear what you say…” was Sahara’s response.

“Sahara!!! Go Clean Up Those Toys immediately!” Grandmouse was very cross and her voice sounded like it too.

“I can’t Grandmouse, I have a sore tummy, sorry about that Grandmouse…”

Sahara went on her way, doing what it was that cheeky mice do — which was not to endeavour in tidying — as she skipped.

"Is my cousin Chanders coming to play with me today?", Sahara asked her Grandmouser.

"No, not today, she is at her new house now. They have just moved there", Grandmouse replied.

"So what? They don't come to visit now?" Sahara questioned.

Grandmouse's eyes and heart filled with laughter till the tears rolled down her face. It was a valid question. How funny was this little mouse? TOO FUNNY.

❁ ❁ ❁

Venturing into the spare bedroom, Grandmouse looked around at the disarray.

There were piles of clothes and piles of books, piles of toys and toys' clothes were strewn about the bedroom.

"What happened in here?", Grandmouse asked a tiny mouse.

"I don't know … but it's not Grandpoo's fault!"

Grandpoo was blamed for most things in Grandmouse's house but on this occasion Sahara was sure it was nothing to do with her funny old Grandpoo.

Sahara loved sleeping in and to be comfortable. A little homebody mouse that was very happy to stay dressed in her pyjamas all day and night.

This could be a challenge to the busy life full of activities and chores all the MouseProuds were involved with throughout the day. Sometimes going out in pyjamas was just not the polite thing to do. This could take some negotiating.

"Come on Darling, we have to go pick up Mazzi Mouse from the School of Mice soon, so get your shoes and socks on and we will need to change you out of those pyjamas", Grandmouse said.

"No... I won't, I will just stay in the mouse mobile", Sahara replied.

She was not interested in changing from her comfortable sleepwear or getting out in the rain to walk to her sister's Mouse classroom.

"I don't think so, you will be changing and you are definitely not staying in the mouse mobile by yourself, for goodness sake Sahara!" was Grandmouse's response.

Whatever would she do with this cheeky little mouse, she wondered?

"I love you, but you smell like an acorn".

"*You* smell like an acorn".

Sahara was busying herself with beauty products one day. She liked spending time with Aunty, painting nails different colours.

Styling her "Rapunzel-like" hair up to look like a fairy tale princess today, her look could change regularly because as all little mice know, there are a lot of fairy tale princesses to choose from and they are all very nice.

"I am going to need yellow on this nail, pink on this nail, purple glitter on this nail and that golden-coloured green on my toenails, thank you Aunty", Sahara requested.

"Sure!" Aunty Clarice replied and set about colouring those tiny little nails.

Once finished, Sahara was very pleased with her new nails, shaking them dry and holding them out to display. All while her favourite Aunt brushed and styled her very mouse-brown hair fashionably high into a bun, with pink clips, which was very becoming on Sahara.

Sahara insisted on seeing herself in a mirror after camera shots from all angles had been taken. Sahara took posing for photographs extremely seriously.

A little mouse must always, always pose nicely and smile, regardless of whether you have just been crying over not wanting to have mousey sleep.

When a camera was present, all mice must turn towards it and give a parmesan smile happily, even when covered in chocolate or spaghetti sauce or wearing biscuit in your hair, with raspberry jam helping it stick up nicely.

She also insisted on quality photography: only the good photos or gross expressions, such as showing a mouth full of chewed-up food, could stay on file permanently. When displaying photos in an album, a mouse must use her little fingers to present the pictures in their best light, waving them over and explaining the scene graciously.

Standing in front of the mirror admiring the changes, she announced with great satisfaction: "Brilliant!!!"

Aunty Clarice was pleased that Sahara was clearly impressed with her presentation.

Me Too...

Sahara was feeling ratty and unwell.

Everyone knew when Sahara MouseProud was unwell, she was very clear about expressing this ill feeling.

Grumpy and sniffly.

It was in the middle of a cold night that Sahara decided to make her way down the long corridor to her Mice parents' bedroom, to wake up her mother.

"What is it, Darling?", Mother asked her tiny Mouse with messy hair and a grumpy expression.

"My ear aches, I think my bed is hurting it, so I have to sleep in your bed with you" was her little reply.

So Sahara climbed into the bed and slept soundly with arms and legs in all directions, across her parents, in a bed that didn't seem to affect her ear-ache.

A Sister's Things

Aunty Clarice had presents for her special, lovely niece, Mazzi. One day, she overheard she had been unwell and thought a present may help cheer her up.

"Here you are, Mazzi, a present to help you feel better", Aunty said as she gave it over to her eldest niece.

Mazzi was delighted; she loved getting presents as most of us do, especially when feeling down. Just what the doctor ordered.

"I don't feel wary (very) well too?" Sahara said, letting out little coughs and holding her forehead to demonstrate this need for a cheer-up gift.

"Oh really Darling, well will I have to get you something also?"

"Yes" was Sahara's reply, before going on in great detail about her day.

As Mousey sisters go, Sahara and her older sister had a fun-loving relationship. They laughed, they cried, they argued, they crossed over into each other's rooms and if you were Sahara, you kept all your dolls in good condition but experimented on your sister's.

Many a toy or hat had been affected by the curious nature of this tiny mouse.

Just quietly, she could be found sitting in her sister's bedroom, up on a chair at her office desk, using all the pens and stationery available, which were previously all neat and tidy but now well-used and not in their original place.

A box that once held mice shoes was now empty, except for two small toy figurines that had found a new home. Toys needed homes, apparently shoes did not. Drawers held little surprises here and there, much unexpected.

Sahara's toy kitten could often be found in random places, such as inside hats or in the kitchen oven.

Why this happened? Maybe it was her mischievous imaginary friend, Lupin? Maybe her imaginary ballet friends had been over for cup-of-tea dates?

Who knew why?

But her older sister will not at all be pleased to find her dolls had been drawn on in dark patterns, in different places, on different body parts.

None of Sahara's dolls needed this artwork, only her sisters.

"What is going on here Sahara? Why are there patterns on this doll's face?", Mother MouseProud asked.

"It's a tattoo…", Sahara replied.

"Really? Wow…well your sister will not be very happy; you have given all her dolls tattoos…"

"Who cares? I don't care…I love it." This reflected Sahara's feelings on most subjects.

What could one say about this? The tattoos would be permanent.

The arguments would erupt, the older sister crying loudly in dismay or arguing with her mischievous little sister with little regard for the welfare of the toys.

"You are so selfish!"

"No! You are so, so selfish!"

"You are NOT the boss, I am the Boss!"

"No, you're not the Boss of me, I am the Boss of you."

"Burp"

"You are GROSS Sahara!"

"NO, YOU ARE GROSS."

"I just did a burp from my butt", was Sahara's reply.

"That is truly disgusting!"

"You are disgusting. I am telling mum on you."

"Who cares?"

"You have to care! Mother says you are not allowed to say WHO cares?"

"Who cares?! I don't care…", Sahara said as she silently walked on into another adventure.

Sitting together, Grandmouse and tiny Sahara chatted about the people going by. Along comes a bicycle with a father peddling his daughter along in a bicycle seat. It looked like fun to Grandmouse.

"How good is that Sahara? Would you like your Father to take you for a ride in a seat like that?"

"If my father did that, I would be so embarrassed", Sahara replied.

So it is a 'no' from you? Grandmouse thought.

One thing all cousins would agree on was their love of singing and dancing to music. All types appealed to them, but mainly pop songs with a lot of 'ooh' and 'ahhs' or yelling statements with a rock beat.

Mazzi loved pop and jazz, Chanders loved Rock 'n Rolling and ballet, Sahara loved hip hop funky dancing with a lot of butt wiggles and flicking her paws around like she was shooing mosquitoes.

All sang as loudly as they could in the back of the car to the Mouse List compiled by their music-loving parents.

They sang into hair brushes, toys, or mouse Karaoke microphones, with feeling and with wild hand movements.

A strong fist pump in the air or an arm raised to the sky was Sahara's famous action. She could be found doing this regularly at any time, dressed wearing her pyjamas… because as we know, Sahara liked to be comfortable when she performed her concerts in the lounge room.

Giving it a true performance meant you had to use your whole body to sing to an audience, whether truly in front of you or imagined.

Aunty Clarice fully encouraged this. She always loved to sing along loudly to upbeat songs on the way home from school or to music lessons. Dance concerts and plays also made for a joyfully excellent event.

Music was a favourite thing of all the MouseProuds; dancing was also especially loved by all.

Conversations with Sahara were often short and sharp. Aunty thought it was part of her appeal. SHE cut the cheese swiftly and precisely.

No time to waste as there were games to play and businesses like her Café or Ice cream shop to run, and then of course dealing with her troublesome imaginary friends… that disastrous Lupin and his sister Lupay.

To cut back on the use of unnecessary words, Sahara could be heard chatting away to whoever was in her presence with:

"What you said?"

"What is your name?" "What is its name?"

"Ahhh No"

"Well actually…I don't know"

"Minished! (Finished)"

"I don't know…why you asking me for?" She said this even if she started the line of questioning.

"Do you think this is such a great idea?... Hmmm?"

"What a silly little mouse…"

"Let's Go!"

"I am out" "I am in"

"Green? Super Green?" "I am thinking…"

"TA DA!"

"Have we been here long enough yet Grandmouse?" "Let's just go…"

"So, So Weird"

"How embarrassing"

"Just get over it…" "Whaaatttt?"

"Louder!"

"It's a DANCE PARTY!"

"Where are my shoes?"

Of late, Sahara had taken to speaking in accents and asking, "Hey? Are you a DAWGG?"

To her father's dismay she would enter the room and say: "What's up Dawgg?"

Aunty Clarice had her favourite cheeky sayings that she loved hearing Sahara say. Cheeky Sahara would sing answers sometimes.

"What are you a-saying?...." Sahara would sing.

Aunty would reply, "You know what I am saying…"

"NO I don't…"

Sahara would sing answer, "Yes you do..."

Aunty would sing back, "I don't know what you are talking about?"

Sahara would answer back.

Then she would turn her back and walk swiftly into another room to meet up with her toys or tea set.

Aunty Clarice had names for all her nieces; Aunty had pet names for most things and people she really liked. Aunty was just wacky fun with her nieces and nephew Jester MouseProud.

Sometimes she had to be serious because she worked for the Mouse Hospital but she was always happy to see her little cheeky nieces and nephew.

Mazzi was her special little lovely, Chanders was her gorgeous little lovely and Sahara was her beautiful little lovely. . . but if you asked Sahara, she would just say:

“I am just Sahara, not lovely!”

She was just Sahara, that is all, nothing more was needed to define who she was.

Sometimes Sahara did not want to talk to people, she was shy, or unsure of whom she was with. It did not last long but it could happen several times a month.

Sometimes Sahara played a silent game. She didn't want to talk so she just pointed directions and it was like a mystery tour. She would point to her ear muffs and her father would help her with them. She would point to her food or drink and he would be handy and pass them to her.

She would demand to be carried and her father would carry her. He was a really kind father who understood she just needed to play the game of no words.

It was an anti-social Sahara that walked in hesitantly to mouse day camp. She really was not in the mood for mice today but having her favourite teacher there would ease the tension a bit.

"Good morning Mrs MouseProud, how is our Sahara today?", one of the teachers asked.

"Mmm, we are not really very friendly this morning but she will warm up when she meets up with her usual teacher", Mrs MouseProud said optimistically, hoping her little mouse's mood may lighten.

"Oh...um... well, there has been a change with that; Barbara LittleMouseHen will be taking over Sahara's class..."

"Really?"

"Hi! I am Barbara! Nice to meet you." Barbara smiled cheerfully.

Sahara looked her new teacher up and down with a disgusted expression, clearly this day was just getting worse. All she wanted was to be in her pyjamas at GrandMouse's house. Was that too much to ask?

"You're not Caroline!", she muttered to the teacher and looked at her mother with her stink eye expression. Not acceptable to Sahara at all. Caroline had better show up next time or Sahara was out…

❁ ❁ ❁

"Why don't you want to go back to see Mouse Camp, Honey?", GrandMouse asked her youngest grandmouse.

"They are Nasty!" was the quick reply. "Let's GO! I'm out…"

"Where do you want to go then?", Grandmouse asked.

"I don't know? Why you asking me for?"

"Well maybe because it was your idea?"

"What do you want for lunch today darling?", Grandmouse asked, trying to change the subject.

"Fish and Chips!" was the reply.

"Ok, what did you have for lunch at Mouse Day Camp yesterday? Was it nice?" Grandmouse was hoping it was not Fish and Chips.

The answer was worse than she had thought.

"Very yukky, disgusting brown stuff…" was Sahara MouseProud's reply.

GrandMouse was at a loss as to what this disgusting brown stuff, possibly the most disgusting thing Sahara had ever eaten could well be? It would remain a mystery.

Sometimes Sahara forgot the need to use her lady-like manners. This was one of those times... "Burp!"

"Oh my goodness, what a loud noise, did you cover your mouth?", Aunty asked.

"No, I just did this… BURP!"

As Sahara walked off cutely, Aunty Clarice shook her head at her youngest niece. *What would she do next?* she thought.

Sahara's dad was a fixer, he fixed things, or so he said. Sahara was not as convinced he really did much except look busy in his working dad clothes.

He left working materials wherever he happened to be and looked like he had been climbing in and out of mouse holes all day... but she had doubts that any real jobs were done.

A day like every other and her father was looking busy, carrying a ladder, climbing up and down it and checking a light, putting it back, checking something else and putting it back. This went on for some time and her Grandmouse was watching the goings on.

"What are you doing in there Sahara?", Mother asked.

"Nothing..." was the little reply.

"Is dad fixing the lights for you?"

"Nah, he is just up the ladder stuffing around..." was Sahara's personally observant reply.

Both Mother MouseProud and GrandMouse burst into laughter but Sahara's dad was not impressed by her comment. What a VERY cheeky mouse she was!

Sahara didn't believe the rules were truly meant for her, how could they be? That just did not go with what she planned throughout her miscellaneous pyjama-wearing day.

If there was something that she wanted or didn't really feel she wanted to do, she would just give you a look, so sweetly and say:

"Me a Baby"

This statement excused whatever it was you had objected to her doing. This excuse was used very often, along with blatant ignoring of being chastised.

It was quickly relayed via Sahara from her Mother to her Aunty or Uncle, or from GrandMouse to Grandpoo via Sahara.

"RELAX, settle please?" Mother said to Sahara. Quickly Sahara turned to her Aunty and announced: "U-LAX!"

Aunty Clarice stood by the kitchen bench, stunned; she thought she was relaxed. How did this chaos become her doing?

"Do not tell your Aunty off! I told you to RELAX, you are not the BOSS!" Mother MouseProud scolded.

Later on in the night…

Aunty needed some help with the washing. Aunty was always doing washing or vacuuming, which Sahara was pleased about as she liked to try on different clothes throughout the day and they would need washing.

Sahara helped her Aunty hang clothes, fold clothes, and check clothes in case dirty clothes had been mixed with clean clothes.

"Are they clean?", Aunty asked.

"Sniff, Sniff. Clean." Sahara gave the socks a sniff test and found them fresh smelling, so they must be clean.

Sahara was a great laundry helper; the clothes were sorted in no time.

Shopping was another task Sahara was very efficient in. Often seen whizzing around the Cheese Market with a mini trolley with only a red flag to alert other shoppers and a loud "BEEP! BEEP!" coming past in a blur.

In the trolley was dinner food, such a help for Grandmouse, who ran swiftly close behind her up and down the market aisles. Shopping was zippy zappy fun.

Salmon was a big favourite food on Sahara's list of main food groups, possibly because it was the colour of her favourite hue, pink. This was closely followed by dumplings, fish and chips, cheese, cheese sticks, strawberries, ice cream, fried rice, zim zimmz, cupcakes, and pancakes with syrup. Also, Spaghetti Bolognese, mayonnaise, sushi sushi…and chocolate frogs with a mixture of white and dark chocolate… food glorious food.

Another important food group was Ice Cream.

Ice cream was something Sahara took very seriously. The preparation before going into her mouth was essentially a lot of stirring in the bowl with her tiny pink spoon.

You swirl it, break it down, swirl it again, mix it, swirl it, till all the ice cream ingredients including sprinkles are combined into a creamy custard-like consistency. This was then examined closely by Sahara, dropping from the spoon into the bowl a couple of times before finally eating it all up.

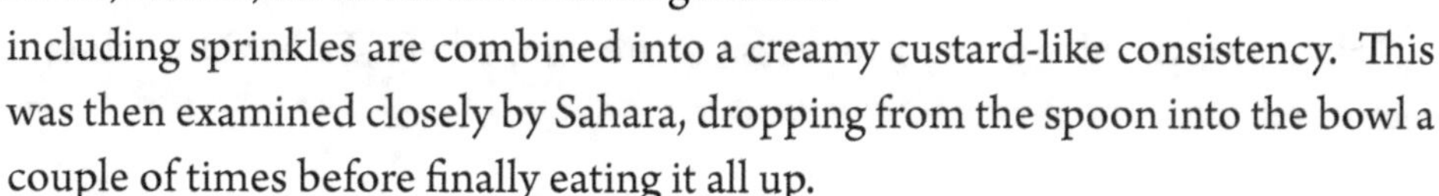

"TA DA!!"

That is the science behind a lot of Sahara's ice cream preparation.

Mr MouseProud was running late, so so late for an important job, but he had been working on grubby work sites and really needed to wash the dirt off.

As he finished in the soapy shower, he noticed that all the towels had been taken and he would need some towels. He thought, *I better call out for assistance.*

Sahara was nearby playing with her dolls when her father called out to her, "Little mouse, please go find me some towels to dry myself off with?"

"Sure", she said and wandered off into the other room where towels would no doubt be very evident to be seen and carried back by Sahara to her shivering Dad.

Time went by and no towels had come. Where was this little mouse and why were there no towels?

"Honey, you need to get me a towel as I am freezing in here", Father MouseProud requested.

"Sahara has gone to collect one for you" was Mother MouseProud's reply.

"You know she will not come back; please go find me a towel to dry off with?"

Sahara was found in her toy room playing with her favourite dolls in the middle of the area happily, oblivious to her father's shivering in the mouse shower.

"Sahara? Your father asked you to bring him a towel, why did you not return with one?", Mother asked.

"I couldn't find them" was Sahara's calm reply. She went on playing with her toys and creating scenarios in which they could star.

The end so far…

www.ingramcontent.com/pod-product-compliance
Lightning Source LLC
Chambersburg PA
CBHW081359090726
47908CB00011B/2736